Dedicated to the memory of Liesl Joseph Loeb and the other passengers of the MS St. Louis who showed extraordinary courage and to my late parents, Milton and Lillian Perlman Krasner, who taught me to recognize such courage and to stand up for what I believe in.

Text copyright © 2014 Barbara Krasner
Illustrations copyright © 2014 Avi Katz

All rights reserved. This book may not be reproduced in whole or in part, by any means without the express written permission of Gihon River Press, except in the case of brief excerpts for the purposes of reviews and articles. For inquires and permissions contact:

Gihon River Press
P.O. Box 88
East Stroudsburg PA 18301
917 612 8857
gihonriverpress@msn.com

ISBN: 978-0-9890841-6-1
Library of Congress Cataloging-in-Publication Data pending

Printed in China

Barbara Krasner

Liesl's Ocean Rescue

Based on a True Story

Illustrations by Avi Katz

GIHON RIVER PRESS
East Stroudsburg PA 18301
2014

Rheydt, Germany, November 9, 1938

"What fun we had last night," Josef Joseph said. "It was the best birthday yet."

"You're very old now, Father," Liesl said. "You're 56!" Mother placed breakfast plates in front of them.

Insistent knocking interrupted their conversation. Two men with high, polished boots, black uniforms, and red armbands bearing the Nazi swastika burst in. They rifled through Father's papers on his desk.

"You are under arrest," they said. They dragged Father out the door. Liesl stood there in shock. He couldn't have done anything wrong.

Mother frantically called her friends. All the men of Rheydt were arrested.

Liesl had finally fallen asleep that night when Mother broke into her room and wrenched her out of bed. Thunderous bangs and crashes on the first floor made Liesl's heart pound. Mother's tight grasp and her own terror kept her still.

In the morning, they tiptoed to the first floor. It looked like it had been blasted by a bomb—the gas range had been yanked from the wall. Torn books, broken tables, chairs, and china lay sprawled on the floor.

All the glass lay shattered.

Elsewhere in Rheydt, vandals burned the synagogue and destroyed Jewish businesses. Kristallnacht, the papers called it, "Night of the Broken Glass." It was part of a deliberate two-day attack against Jews all over Germany.

A policeman called and told Mother that Father was all right. He had been taken to the local jail.

"We have to get you to safety," Mother said. She packed Liesl off to a friend who lived in another city about an hour away.

When Father was released from jail a month later, both he and Mother visited Liesl. He looked tired, but at least they were a family again.

"We have to leave Germany," Father said back in Rheydt. They were living in an apartment. Their house belonged to someone else now.

"Forever?" Liesl asked.

"Yes" said Father. But Father could always make things all right. And he did.

On May 13, 1939, the smokestacks of the MS St. Louis boomed as the ship pulled up anchor in Hamburg's harbor.

The Josephs joined nearly 1,000 other German-Jewish passengers bound for Havana, Cuba—and then, America.

"My name is Liesl," she said to two girls on deck, her checkerboard under her arm. "Want to play?" She was good at checkers. Sometimes she even beat Father.

"We're Renate and Ruth," the girls said. Liesl let them win. At home, she rarely had friends her own age to play with.

"Can I bang the gong for you?" Liesl asked the cabin steward. Striking the gong, she called everyone to dinner.

On the ship, Liesl could eat whatever she wanted. She could walk freely around the ship and see movies in the recreation room whenever they played. Back in Germany, she could only eat rationed bread and eggs. And Jews like Liesl and her family weren't allowed to stroll in the park, walk on the sidewalk, or go to the movies.

"Can I push the buttons for you? Liesl asked the elevator operator when he wanted to take a break. She loved to see them light up.

One day, Captain Schroeder invited Father for a tour of the bridge. Liesl tagged along. The captain said, "There's going to be trouble in Havana." He asked Father to head up a committee that would speak on his behalf to the passengers. "You're a lawyer," he said. "You know how to calm people in bad situations." Father agreed.

Liesl knew Father would make everything all right.

Two weeks after leaving Germany, the St. Louis steamed into Havana harbor. Father took Liesl up to the deck to see her new home. The entire city was lit up—palm trees and pastel-colored houses. It was like paradise.

Everyone crowded the hallways with their luggage. But armed Cubans in uniforms boarded the ship and didn't allow anyone to leave.

Father and his committee huddled in the radio room, sending cablegrams for help.

On the third day in the harbor a seaplane arrived with a New York lawyer, sent by the American Jewish Joint Distribution Committee to negotiate the passengers' release.

"This lawyer," Father told Liesl, "will make everything all right."

But after nearly a week in the harbor, Captain Schroeder announced the Cuban president insisted they leave Havana.

The next day passengers asked Father, "What will happen to us?"

They pleaded, "Don't let the ship go back to Germany. We'll be taken to the concentration camps and killed."

They insisted, "Tell us we'll be safe."

Thousands of cars along the shore and more than ten police boats escorted them to sea.

The ship criss-crossed between Cuba and Florida for three days. Father did not return to the cabin until after Liesl fell asleep. By the time she woke up, he was gone again.

Father looked so tired as he stood next to the captain in the social hall. He said, "The ship received orders to go back to Germany."

The passengers chanted, "We will not return…we must not die…we will not return."

Liesl moped around the ship. She didn't even feel like playing checkers. "Can I help, Father?" she asked.

After that, when Captain Schroeder needed a bulletin posted to help calm the passengers, Liesl volunteered.

When Father called a special meeting of the passengers, Liesl banged the gong to call everyone into the social hall.

When other children sulked, Liesl pulled out the checkers. "Everything will turn out all right, you'll see," she said.

Father said someone new took charge of finding a safe place for them: Mr. Morris Troper, head of the Joint's Paris office. He and Father exchanged lots of telegrams.

On June 12, Father received the glorious message: "Final arrangements…completed… Happy inform you governments of Belgium Holland France and England cooperated magnificently…"

Liesl banged the gong so loud it drowned out the ship's orchestra.

Because Father was head of the committee and because June 17 was Liesl's eleventh birthday, she received the special honor of greeting Mr. Troper when he came on board. Father helped her write her speech.

On the morning of June 17, Liesl and the nearly 200 other children lined the ship's hallway. The adults crowded the rails. The tug boat carrying Mr. Troper and his helpers pulled up. Everyone waved, shouting, "G-d bless you," as he boarded.

Liesl stepped forward and said in German:

"Dear Mr. Troper, The children on the St. Louis are most thankful to you for rescuing them out of deepest despair. They are praying for G-d's blessing for you. Unfortunately, flowers do not grow on board; we would have liked to hand you a bouquet of flowers."

"But I have a bouquet for you," Mr. Troper said. He leaned down and gave her two dozen roses. "I heard you've been a big help around here. And happy birthday!"

"Mr. Troper," Liesl said, "Saving us is the best present ever."

Author's Note

I first learned of the St. Louis and its failed attempts to land safely in the United States either from my Hebrew school teachers, who were Holocaust survivors, or my parents. Even as a child, I found this story hard to understand. How could America, with our Statue of Liberty and her words of "Give me your tired, your poor, your huddled masses yearning to breathe free," refuse these 900 people refuge?

The flight from one country to another for freedom continues today. That is why I thought it was important to tell this story.

Liesl Joseph and her family came to America in September 1940 and settled in Philadelphia, Pennsylvania. She always liked to draw and became a graphic designer and artist. She could recite her speech to Morris Troper more than sixty years later. She said of her experience on the St. Louis, "We have learned that we cannot stand by idly and watch people being bullied, harassed, and punished for no reason. We have to take action and if we can't handle a situation by ourselves, we have to go and get help and end a situation that is harming other people—other kids, other grownups." She died in August 2013.

I have many people to thank in my efforts to research and write this story. First, I'd like to humbly and affectionately thank Liesl Joseph Loeb, whom I interviewed at her home in Elkins Park, Pennsylvania and corresponded with through phone calls and emails. She was a remarkable person.

I owe gratitude to the staff at the various archives and organizations I consulted: American Jewish Joint Distribution Committee in New York City; Museum of Jewish Heritage, also in New York; and U.S. Holocaust Memorial Museum in Washington, DC.

I also thank Dr. Severin Hochberg for vetting an early manuscript, Scott Miller of the U.S. Holocaust Memorial Museum for vetting the final manuscript, Lenore Shapiro for her St. Louis materials, and Ann Ingalls and Anna Olswanger for helping me shape the manuscript.

For More Information

DVDs

American Joint Distribution Committee, *Bound for Nowhere*, 1939
Original footage

Bahari, Maziar, *The Voyage of the St. Louis*, Galafilm, 2006
A mix of original footage and survivor testimony

Holocaust Memorial Foundation of Illinois and Loyola University of Chicago, *The Double Crossing: The Voyage of the St. Louis*, Ergo Media, 1994.
A mix of original footage and survivor testimony

A Living Memorial to the Holocaust—Museum of Jewish Heritage, *Memories of Kristallnacht: More than Broken Glass*, Ergo Media, 1990.

Books

Buff, Fred. *Riding the Storm Waves: The St. Louis Diary of Fritz Buff.* Margate, New Jersey: ComteQ Publishing, 2009.

Selected Bibliography

Interviews and email correspondences with Liesl Joseph Loeb throughout 2010 and 2011.

Primary Documents and Documentaries

American Joint Distribution Committee. "Bound for Nowhere." 1939.

American Joint Distribution Committee Archives
- Memorandum on S.S. "St. Louis" – HAPAG, June 27, 1939.
- "The Voyage of the 'St. Louis'," June 15, 1939.

U.S. Holocaust Memorial Museum
The Joseph Family Collection, 2003.58
- "From the Diary of Josef Joseph, Chairman of the Passenger Committee on Board the S.S. St. Louis—June 1938[sic]"

Bahari, Maziar. "The Voyage of the St. Louis." Galafilm, 2006.

Buff, Fred. Riding the *Storm Waves: The St. Louis Diary of Fritz Buff*. Margate, New Jersey: ComteQ Publishing, 2009.

USC Shoah Foundation Institute for Visual History and Education. Video recordings accessed through the U.S. Holocaust Memorial Museum, Washington, D.C. and YouTube
(Liesl's testimony: http://www.youtube.com/watch?v=0h5rfmyFL6Q)

Books

Ogilvie, Sarah A. and Miller, Scott. *Refuge Denied: The St. Louis Passengers and the Holocaust*. Madison: University of Wisconsin Press, 2006.

Thomas, Gordon and Witts, Max M. Voyage of the Damned. London: Motorbooks, 1974